The JoJo Bow & Bow Show Show

Our Wild Adventures

SCHOLASTIC INC.

Hey, everyone! It's me,  JoJa!

I love having fun, and I've had some craaaaazy adventures! I'm so excited to show you some awesome moments from my wild life!

But I couldn't do it without my best friend—who is also the thing I love most of all . . .

(Flip the page to see who!)

My dog, BowBow!

You all know that BowBow is the most adorable dog on the planet, right?

But she's so much more than that!

I ♥ U

BowBow has a whole secret life. She takes my socks while I'm sleeping, and she and her dog pals have sock fashion shows!

She's also SUPER talented. This dog knows how to entertain a crowd!

BowBow even owns a business making dog onesies! #smartestdogeva

I love my BFF (best furry friend)!

My Room!

BowBow and I love to hang out in my awesome room. It's the best place to kick back and relax after a busy day. Check it out!

Here's where I sleep! #bedtimebow

You can never have enough sparkle!

LOL

There's even room for a spot of tea here!

OMG

BowBow's Canine Condo

BowBow has a place of her own—a secret doggy hideout. I call it her Canine Condo. It's craaaaazy amazing! BowBow is living the life!

There's even a kibble bar!

100% LOVE IT!

Anyone need a doggy decorator?

My Hometown!

NEBRASKA

omaha

I love Omaha! It's the largest city in Nebraska, and no matter where I go and what I do, it will always be my hometown.

Five fun facts about Omaha:

1 Omaha has its own fashion week! Ooh la la!

2 TV dinners were invented there.

3 Omaha has a huge indie rock scene.

4 The zoo has the largest indoor rain forest in the country.

5 It's the hometown of Fred Astaire!

The last time I had a concert in Omaha, so many family members and friends came!

BowBow was especially excited to see Denny the mailman. She chased him all over the stage! Hilarious!

Whoa! Whoa!

Things I Love!

The best adventures are full of things I love! Things like . . .

Bows!

Dancing!

JACOB & EINSTEIN'S
TEEN CUIS

Singing!

15

Pizza sticks!

Onesies!

Pizza sticks wearing onesies!

The best colors: rainbow, pink, and glitter—in that order!

And the thing I love most of all . . .

BowBow, the cutest dog in the whole universe!

OMG

17

Things BowBow Loves!

And let's not forget the things that BowBow loves. She's a pup who knows what's cool! She loves things like . . .

LOL

Chicken-flavored toothpaste!

The *Jurassic Bark* movies!

Bingo!

Doing the limbo! (How low low can BowBow go go?)

Naps!

TTYL

Peanut butter-hot dog-supreme
kibble with extra bacon bits!

Squeaky ANYTHING—even furniture!

21

Our Friends
(Humans AND Pets!)

BowBow and I have been having a blast making tons of new friends lately on our adventures! We love hanging out with humans *and* pets. Here are some of our besties!

Kyra & Hamela

Kyra is a sleek fashionista with a sweet sense of style!

Her pet pig, Hamela, has a snout for fashion . . . and is an amazing tap dancer!

I ♥ U

Grace & Georgi

Grace is from the UK. She's super artistic and loves unicorns!

Her dog, Georgi, can howl a cool tune!

Miley & Dusty

Miley is a fabulous DJ, dropping next-level beats all over the neighborhood!

Miley's pony, Dusty, has some serious country line dancing moves!

Jacob & Einstein

Jacob is a crazy-good cook, and loves whipping up new recipes in the kitchen!

Jacob's rascally raccoon, Einstein, likes to help out on Jacob's baking show . . . and forage for ingredients!

Beans

Beans is the doggy next door, and BowBow's longtime rival! Beans and BowBow didn't see tail to tail at first, but now they're mostly friendly . . . even though Beans can still be a grouch sometimes!

 We're so lucky to have all these great friends to share amaaaaazing adventures with!

Epic Adventures
We've Had Together!

We gathered all our pet pals for a fierce but friendly competition!

Hamela *tapped* into her potential with an awesome tap dance!

28

Georgi yodeled like a pro!

Dusty used her high-top hooves in a crazy country line dance!

And Einstein spun five plates of delicious food like it was no big deal!

Beans was a grumpy judge, but she came around in the end. Bows for everyone!

29

skydiving

This adventure literally defied gravity—we went skydiving with Kyra and Hamela, for realz!

These two are always fierce in the face of something scary!

Kyra even designed us super-special flight suits!

BowBow was scared, but we knew we could do it—together!

We showed our flair in the air!

It was our most amazing, fun, and fashionable adventure EVER!

Backpacking BowBow

Backpack shopping at the mall with Miley and Dusty got cray cray!

Backpack Paradise is the best. It's like being on a tropical vacation, but with backpacks instead of sand!

BowBow found a backpack that was as soft as a giant marshmallow!

When Miley spotted this epic bow-shaped backpack, I got a little distracted!

Then someone carried off the marshmallow backpack . . . with BowBow sleeping inside!

It was a wild chase, but I finally lured BowBow back with her fave chicken-flavored toothpaste . . . whew!

Crazy Crafts!

Super-Epic Bow

BowBow and I love a good craft, and so do all of our friends!

We had all the pets over to make bows one day.

Nothing was going as planned! Everyone kept arguing. Yikes!

Teamwork to the rescue! All of the pets worked together to make one SUPER-EPIC BOW!

BowBow gave it two paw prints of approval, and I thought it was totally amaaaaazing!

Uni-Crafts!

Grace and Georgi are all about unicorns, and they invited us over for uni-crafts!

Or is it crafty-corns?

Grace is an expert unicorn painter! She has tons of fans.

Georgi was worried that Grace would want a unicorn for a pet . . . instead of her!

Grace did a special painting of Georgi as a unicorn—a Georgicorn!

Our glittery uni-crafts were uni-tastic!

BowBow's Dream

BowBow had the craziest dream one night. She dreamed she was a unicorn who lived on a rainbow with donuts and lollipops that wore bows and sang!

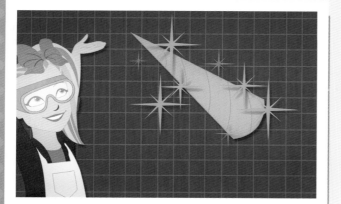

I always say, "If you can dream it, you can do it!" But how would I make BowBow's totally crazy dream come true?

It was time for a Do-It-Yourself Dream!

I made a bow rainbow
and a glittery horn
for BowBow, and my
mom brought home
donuts and lollipops!

I even made the
donuts and lollipops
sing!

It was a doggy
dream come true!

Things We've Learned
on Our Adventures

The Best Things in Life Happen When You Work Together!

We made a huge mess helping Jacob and Einstein celebrate the hundredth episode of their baking show. But we worked together to clean it up—and have fun, too!

BowBow and Beans were competing to sell different dog onesies—but when they combined their ideas, their sales really took off!

When all the pets worked together to make one giant bow, it was AMAZINGLY EPIC!

BowBow rocked the doggy fashion show wearing
my bedtime bow!

I used my itsy-bitsy bow to make myself tiny
and visit BowBow's Canine Condo!

I gave Beans a super-duper special bow for judging our pet pageant, and it totally made her feel like a winner, too!

Bow-tastic!

LOL

BowBow and I work hard to make our dreams come true—and so can you!

Maybe we'll go to outer space one day!

Or become secret agents!

No matter what, we'll do it in style!

And it will be a wild ride, that's for sure!

45